That's What I Am

by Kersten Richter

Illustrated by Sharon Grey

This one is for the boys...

My sons, my father, and most of all, my husband.

ISBN: 978-0-9972581-0-3

Luke woke up one morning and came down the stairs, yawning and rubbing his eyes.

"Why, Luke," his father said, "You look like a bear, just waking up from a long winter's nap."

"That's what I am, Dad," said Luke. "I am a bear, sleepy and hungry."
He yawned again, as he sat down to eat his breakfast.

After breakfast Luke headed up the stairs to get dressed and then he ran back down.
"Whoa there!" his father called.
"You are just like a race horse, charging from the starting gate."

"That's what I am, Dad," said Luke. "I am a horse and I'm going to win the big race."

He ran down the hall and out the back door.

Outside, Luke zoomed around the yard.
"Luke," his father called out, "You look just like an airplane, soaring high up in the sky."

"That's what I am, Dad," said Luke. "I am an airplane, flying off to faraway places."

Luke spent the afternoon playing in his sand box.
"Vroom, chugga-chug, beep beep."

"Luke," his father said, "you sound just like a big dirt mover."

"That's what I am," said Luke. "I am a big dirt mover and I have to make the road so that the cars can get through."

He built a two-lane highway across his sand box, just the right size for his cars.

During his bath, Luke splashed about, spilling water everywhere.

"Luke," his father said, "You are like a little otter, splashing around in the water."

"That's what I am, Dad," Luke said. "I am an otter and I'm chasing the fish."

He splashed around until bath time was over.

After his bath, Luke got his pajamas on and curled up in the chair.

"Luke," his dad said, "You look like a sleepy little kitten, curled up in the sunlight. You'd better head up to bed."

"That's what I am, Dad," said Luke.
"I am a sleepy kitten who wants to go to bed."

And so his father carried him upstairs and tucked him into bed.

Later that night, Luke came back down the stairs, blanket in hand and rubbing his eyes. "Dad," he said. "I got scared."

"Well," his father said, "You look like a little boy who needs a cuddle."
"That's what I am," said Luke. "I am your little boy and I need to snuggle."
He climbed into his father's lap and curled up tight.

After a few minutes, he sat up.
"Dad, do you know what I like being best of all?"
"What's that, Luke?"

"I like being your little boy."

Then he burrowed back into his father's arms and went to sleep.

Kersten lives in Minnesota with her husband and boys. She enjoys morning walks with her mother and never acts her age. You can find her on Facebook at https://www.facebook.com/kerstenrichterbooks/ This is Kersten's second book.

Sharon lives in the Black Hills of South Dakota with her husband and three kids who, like Luke, LOVE to pretend every day. Her son, Ethan, mostly pretends he is a wrecking ball, and does so very convincingly. She also has two cats and a dog. They do not pretend to approve of Ethan, but have learned to stay out of his way. She has been an illustrator for nine years, and has created about two dozen books

29546637R00020

Made in the USA
Middletown, DE
23 February 2016